THANK YOU

Lucille (Granny) O'Brien for giving me **Folklore & Legends of Trinidad and Tobago** all those years ago. Whether you know it or not, you started me down the path to creating this book.

Ashleigh Staton for helping me see this project to the very end and for being a loving yet honest critic along the way.

Eljon Wardadly for being the person that helped me get the ball rolling.

Special thanks to Trinidad and Tobago. Be it for my endlessly loving family and friends that reside within its borders or its rich and vastly beautiful culture, the land of my birth will forever feed my spirit and my imagination.

Supporting independent writers, artists, and other creatives is an important part of creating a more vibrant and colorful world for us all. Thank you for supporting the indie creation of this book and for not reproducing or using it in any manner without written permission of the copyright owner (Daniel J. O'Brien), except for the use of short quotations in a book review. Send press and permissions inquiries to rights@rowhousepublishing.com or Wheat Penny Press, PO Box 210, New Egypt, NJ 08533.

Second edition January 2022; Published by Wheat Penny Press; Printed in the United States
Library of Congress Cataloging-in-Publication Data Available Upon Request
ISBN: 978-1-7369497-2-6; electronic book ISBN: 978-1-7369497-5-7

Fonts used in the design of this book: Cherry and Sassoon Primary
Illustrations were created with graphite on paper and were colored and composed in Clip Studio Paint

The Carnival Prince is an original modern folklore picture book for ages 7-10

Wheat Penny Press is an imprint of Row House Publishing

Daniel J. O'Brien is a Trinidadian-born author, illustrator, and creator living in New York with his wife, Ashleigh, and their dog, Obbie. Daniel holds a BFA in Illustration from The School of Visual Arts.

 **www.danielostudios.com**

THE
CARNIVAL
PRINCE

Daniel J. O'Brien

Fountaindale Public Library District
300 W. Briarcliff Rd.
Bolingbrook, IL 60440

1

Too Young to Soca

It all started with a loving embrace.

Long ago, during a beautiful **Trinidad** sunset, in a place where the woodland met the surf, **Papa Boi** and **Mama D'Lo**, two ancient and powerful creatures of the islands, sat under the leaves of the **Peewah Tree**.

In the morning, they left behind three eggs.

When the sun rose,
a **Scarlet Ibis** happened upon the eggs.

She sat on them for many days.

A song as sweet as a freshly baked **currant roll** emerged from the first egg and was carried away on a warm **Caribbean** breeze.

The second egg hatched goo as black as **pitch**, and it floated away on the creeping island tides.

The last egg hatched the most unusual thing of all—a full-grown boy!

The Scarlet Ibis fled into the woods in fright,
leaving a trail of feathers and the boy behind her.

The full-grown boy with the dark curls and stubby antlers followed the feathers into the woods all the way to the very frightened Scarlet Ibis.

Feeling sorry for the nearly naked, shivering bird and not wanting to scare her, the boy got to work on a plan.

He grabbed her loose feathers, a few twigs, and some vines and turned them into a Scarlet Ibis costume!

The bird found his disguise so silly that she laughed out loud, setting the boy at ease.

Sharing his talents (and laughter) helped the boy make a new friend.

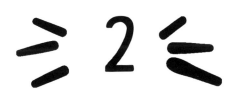

Good Times

The boy and Scarlet Ibis spent their days exploring Trinidad.

Some days they splashed with the manatees in the **Nariva Swamp** until the sun set behind the thick marsh bush.

In the evening, they played games with the ghostly **Douens** in the wild forests of **Trinity Hills**.

Blind Man's Bluff was the eyeless Douens's favorite game.

In the afternoon, the boy would sit and listen to the migrating ducks tell stories. They quacked about places they had visited and about all the unique animals they had seen.

The ducks told stories of places where the water turned so cold that it froze and wild cats grew bigger than men!

The boy made costumes based on the tales that his feathered friends told.

He and his friends paraded jubilantly through the woods, pretending to be the creatures from the stories.

They created quite a scene!

≧3≦

Ah Come Out to Party

Along with all the good of the islands came a fair share of bad.

There were other creatures who roamed the island who were not very nice, like **Dragon** and his **Imp** minions.

They roamed the deepest, most perilous parts of Trinidad, causing nothing but trouble.

On one of his terrifying jaunts, Dragon trapped **Red Howler Monkey** and cut off his tail. Dragon's favorite meal was monkey tail stew.

And he trapped **Porcupine** so he could use her quills for toothpicks!

Dragon was a miserable wretch. He would always find a way to ruin someone else's good time.

Time moved forward and things changed.

The trees grew taller, and the creatures grew older.

The bush shrank, making way for growing towns and cities.

The boy with the stubby antlers stayed the same. But that was fine by the boy. He didn't like change.

He would stand at the edge of the woods, looking out at the new world and feeling nothing but dread.

The boy felt safe in his familiar stomping grounds. The thought of stepping beyond them was scary.

A year passed, and Carnival season came again!

Dressed as a Douen, the boy stood beside his **Jumbee** friends at the edge of the woods, eagerly awaiting the sound of Calypso to fill the streets.

The music started to blare, and the ghosts rushed from the woods to join the Carnival revelers. But the boy froze in place.

The outside world scared him more than ever. The boy climbed to the highest limb of the nearest tree and watched the festivities from afar.

Carnival carried on, and the boy stayed in his tree.

Maybe next year, he thought.

Screams of panic and clouds of smoke rose above the buildings in the middle of town.

A small figure emerged from the metropolis.

It was running right at the boy!

Alarmed, the boy swung down from his perch.

Soon, the boy was able to make out the shape of a man.

In his fiery haste, the man tripped over the boy's costume and hit the floor rolling, putting out the flames that clung to his clothes.

"Are yuh alright?" the boy asked.

The man sprung to his feet, blew his whistle, and boasted...

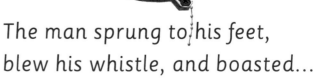

"I am **Deh Midnight Robber!**
Boy, have yuh not heard of me?
I am public enemy one, two, and t'ree!"

"Excuse me," said the boy.

The Midnight Robber ignored him.

"And jus' as sure as deh **Pothound**
has fleas, I am deh only man who
can make hell freeze! I am—"

"Excuse me," repeated the boy.
"What happened in deh town?"

"It's Carnival Monday, boy!

"People came ta celebrate in deh streets,
twistin and turnin' ta hypnotic Calypso beats!

"Followed by his Imps, came deh horrible Dragon Beast!
Emerged from deh deep dark woods, lookin' for a feast!

"Deh people got scared and ran lookin' for covah!
But Deh Midnight Robber stood up ta deh
Dragon ta help his fellow brodda!

"But deh Dragon and deh Imps got
deh best of me, yuh see.
Dose nasty tings set me a blaze!
So of course, I had ta flee!

"Now I stand here tellin' yuh, it is
only a matter of fate.
Yuh believe it, boy. I will soon retaliate!"

Robber noticed the costume at the boy's feet.

"On any other day, I would let yuh be.
But today is yuh lucky day, boy.
How would *you* like ta help *me*?

"We can beat deh Dragon and have a
story ta tell.
Together, we can bid him a *final* farewell!

"Think about deh people being terrorized!
Will yuh let deh Dragon ruin deir day of dancin' in disguise?"

The boy thought of his friends in the forest. He thought about how
Dragon took Monkey's tail and plucked poor Porcupine bald. He didn't
want anyone else to suffer from Dragon's actions.

And so, the boy grabbed his costume and followed his new companion
into town. They walked out of the bush and through the short grass
fields of **Queen's Park Savannah**.

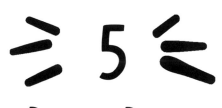

5

Dragon Dance

Soon, the boy and Robber reached the entrance to **St. James**.

The boy could not believe his eyes. A villainous Dragon was dancing and slithering down the road with Imps and chaos in tow.

Some of the devilish Imps ran through the streets with pitchforks while Dragon's flames rained down on the terrified crowd.

Dragon and his minions reveled in the mayhem.

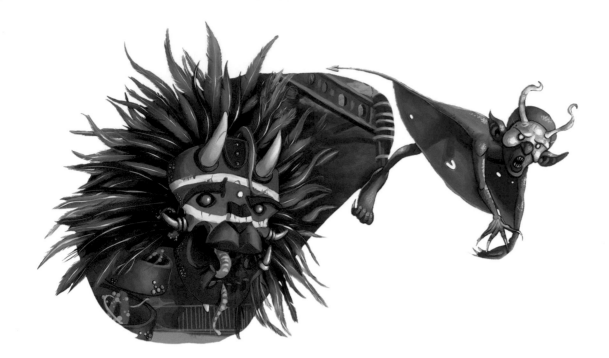

Robber told the boy to put on his costume and hide.

"DRAGON!" yelled Robber.

"Ssso, it is yuh again!" Dragon hissed. "I thought yuh learned yuh lessson deh first time I ssset yuh behind on fiya! Get out of meh way, yuh terrible pretenda, before I barbeque yuh for meh sssuppa!"

But Robber would not back down.

"How dare yuh try ta embarrass me, Dragon!
I am not afraid of yuh threats!
I am here ta rid dis town of yuh *and* yuh little pets!"

Dragon snickered as smoke billowed from his mouth.

Robber realized that he was about to be set on fire again.

"But because I am bored by yuh ridiculous antics,
I have brought yuh a friend dat will surely make yuh panic!

"Dis animal been known ta destroy *whole* villages
by only a mention of its name!
It eats Imps for appetizers and Dragons
for its main!"

"Hahaha! I want ta sssee dis so-called
monstah," Dragon snarled.
"I want ta gaze upon deh ting dat
is sssupposed to be meh bettah."

"Are yuh *sure*?" asked Robber.

"Enough with deh **backchat**, Robber!" Dragon scolded.

But Robber continued with his taunts.

"If yuh lay yuh gaze upon dis mighty beast,
yuh surely gonna be meh partner's feast!

"Come forth from deh shadows,
meh ferocious friend.
Come forth and lead
dese devils to deir end!"

The boy bounded towards Dragon.

"ROAR!" The boy's mighty holler made the Imps cower in fear.

Robber held his breath, and Dragon let loose a terrible laugh.

"Yuh want me ta believe dat dis boy in disguise isss deh one who will ssscare *me* away? Do yuh take me for a fool?"

Dragon and his Imps broke out into a chorus of laughter.

"Get out of meh way, fools!"

With a mighty swoop of his tail, Dragon knocked the boy and Robber into a **Doubles** cart. Food and water spilled everywhere!

Dragon was too busy celebrating his victory to notice the puddle of water at his feet.

But when he *did* notice, Dragon panicked and high-stepped around the puddle to avoid it.

The boy saw what happened and got an idea.

The Midnight Robber sat in the street with his head hung low.

"We tried our best, but our best was not enough.
Deh Dragon saw through yuh disguise and called our bluff."

The boy did not want there to be another reason for him to avoid Carnival next year. He was more determined than ever to beat the horrible Dragon.

He grinned and looked at Robber.

"Deh party not done yet, Mr. Robber! I have a plan.
Tell me—where can we find some ice,
my good man?"

Hearing the boy's confident rhyme made Robber very happy.

He dusted himself off and got ready to listen to the boy's scheme.

6

Fire and Ice

Everyone went to bed sad. Their Carnival Monday was ruined.

But as the people slept, the boy with the stubby antlers and The Midnight Robber worked furiously through the night.

The Carnival revelers crowded **Western Main Road** bright and early the next morning and prayed that Dragon would not appear.

But just as the masqueraders were about to start the music, they saw the monster come slithering down the road.

Everyone cleared the way—everyone but the boy and Robber... and something hidden under a giant tarp.

"Grrrrr," Dragon bellowed.
"Not *you* two again! Why do
allyah continue ta ruin meh fun?"

"Yuh managed ta bess Deh Midnight Robber twice and earn his
respect," the boy answered.
"Because of dat, we made yuh a special gift."

The boy pulled back the tarp to reveal a statue of Dragon that
appeared to be made of fine crystal.

Dragon was very pleased with his present. "Very good, little boy.
I appreciate deh gift. Now move it ta deh side of deh road, so I can
continue on with my celebration."

But the boy would not comply. "Oh my! We never thought about
how ta move yuh statue. I am afraid yuh path is blocked."

The thought of his good time being ruined made Dragon angry.

"How dare yuh get in meh way! I will smash yuh present ta pieces and make ashes of what is left!"

Dragon used his mighty tail to break the statue into a thousand pieces and unleashed a searing flame upon the rubble.

But the crystal did not burn. Instead, it melted! The statue was made of ice!

Dragon's eyes grew as big as saucers, and he let out a deafening scream that shook the ground and rattled the revelers' bones.

Unafraid, the boy stood in front of Dragon and grinned.

Dragon fainted from fear and collapsed into the puddle.

Water was like poison to Dragon's kind.

Dragon awoke to cackling Imps and jeers from the crowd.

Then he heard Robber say, "Now Dragon, yuh bess be goin' on yuh merry way!
Because we all found out what scares yuh on dis very day!"

With his tail tucked between his legs, Dragon took to the sky and escaped over the hills.

His Imps followed behind, laughing at Dragon's misfortune.

The masqueraders ran into the street and lifted the boy and Robber onto their shoulders.

"Thank you, Midnight Robber, and thank you...
Hey, what is yuh name, boy?"

Robber let out a giant belly laugh.

"I think we have all been convinced.
Let's call dis boy **Deh Carnival Prince**!"

The sounds of Steelpan and Calypso rose up and filled the air. The masqueraders celebrated well after the last bit of sunlight disappeared over the horizon.

The only sound louder and more boisterous than the music was the crowd chanting the names of **The Midnight Robber** and their new hero, **The Carnival Prince**.

⇉ Glossary of Terms ⇇

Allyuh (awl·yuh): All of you.

Backchat (bak·chat): Rude or argumentative remarks made in reply to someone in authority. Back talk. Sass.

Blind Man's Bluff (blahynd·manz·bluhf): A version of tag in which the player who is "It" is blindfolded.

Calypso (kuh·lip·soh): It's a style of Afro-Caribbean music that originated in Trinidad and Tobago. The lyrics are usually improvised, and make fun of local people and politics.

Carnival (kahr·ni·vuhl): The season immediately preceding Lent, often observed with merrymaking and a masquerade parade.

Currant roll (kur·uhnt·rohl): A flaky dough filled with cinnamon, brown sugar, and currants.

Caribbean (kar·uh·bee·uhn): pertaining to the Caribs, the Lesser Antilles, or the Caribbean Sea and its islands.

Doubles (duhb·uhlz): A common street food in Trinidad and Tobago. It is a sandwich made with two pieces of flatbread (Baras) filled with curried chickpeas.

Douens (dwens): Known to be souls of children who have died before they were baptized. They wear mushroom-shaped hats and have no faces and their feet are turned backward.

Dragon (drag·uhn): A traditional Carnival character that is a representation of the forces of nature. It is depicted as a fiery beast, that comes to bring mischief and destruction to all. Sometimes, the Dragon is restrained by chains held by imps.

Imp (imp): Also known as Jab-Jab, a traditional Carnival character. He wears a simple devil mask with horns over his face. He usually moves about the crowds, causing mischief.

Jumbee (jum·bee): A type of spirit or demon in the folklore of some Caribbean countries. Jumbee is the common name given to all types of ghosts.

Mama D'Lo (ma·ma·glo): Also known as "Mami Wata" and "Mama Glo," this is the Trinidadian protector of all river animals. She is usually depicted as a beautiful woman with long hair and a serpent's tail.

Midnight Robber (mid·nahyt·rob·er): A traditional Carnival character known for being extravagant and boastful.

Nariva Swamp (nah·ree·vuh·swomp): It is the largest freshwater wetland in Trinidad and Tobago.

Papa Bois (pa·pa·bwah): He is the father or protector of the forest and its inhabitants. Known as a generous figure, he is sometimes described as a half-goat, half-man. He protects the forest and those in his care from harm.

Peewah (pee·wah): Also known as the Peach Palm. It is a fruit native to the tropical forests of South and Central America.

Pitch (pich): A black or dark viscous substance obtained as a residue in the distillation of organic materials and especially tars.

Porcupine (pawr·kyuh·pahyn): The Brazilian porcupine is an endangered species and is protected by law in Trinidad and Tobago. It inhabits tropical forests at elevations up to 1500 m and has a prehensile tail, with the tip curling upward so as to get a better grip on tree branches.

Pothound (pot·hound): A dog of mixed or indeterminate breed. A mutt or mongrel. A street dog.

Queen's Park Savannah (kweenz·pahrk·suh·van·uh): A well-known park in Port of Spain, Trinidad, and Tobago. A lot of Carnival's festivities happen near or around this location.

Red Howler Monkey (red·hou·ler·muhng·kee): A species of monkey known to reside in the forests of Trinidad and Tobago.

Saint James (seynt·jeymz): A district of Port of Spain, Trinidad, and Tobago. The main road is the Western Main Road. It runs from Woodbrook to Cocorite.

Scarlet Ibis (skahr·lit·ahy·bis): The National Bird of Trinidad and Tobago, the red-feathered species of ibis is in the bird family. It inhabits tropical South America and the islands of the Caribbean.

Soca (soh·kah): A style of Caribbean dance music derived from Calypso and American soul music and having a pounding beat.

Steelpan (steel·pan): Also known as "Steel drums" or "Pans" is a musical instrument originating from Trinidad and Tobago. It was one of the many innovations that emerged in the 1930s after a more than 50-year ban on African percussion music. Usually constructed from old oil drums, they're known for their "Ping Pong Ping" sound.

Trinidad (trin·i·dad): An island in the SE West Indies, off the NE coast of Venezuela, formerly a British colony in the Federation of the West Indies, now part of the Republic of Trinidad and Tobago.

Trinity Hills (trin·i·tee·hilz): A range of hills in SE Trinidad. Legend has it that Christopher Columbus named Trinidad after these hills. Columbus had promised to name the next land he discovered after the Holy Trinity.

Western Main Road (wes·tern·meyn·rohd): The main road in Trinidad and Tobago that runs west from Green Corner in downtown Port of Spain, through Saint James, where it is the main thoroughfare until the Military Base in Chaguaramas. It is most notable as the scene of the Hosay, which is held in May or June.

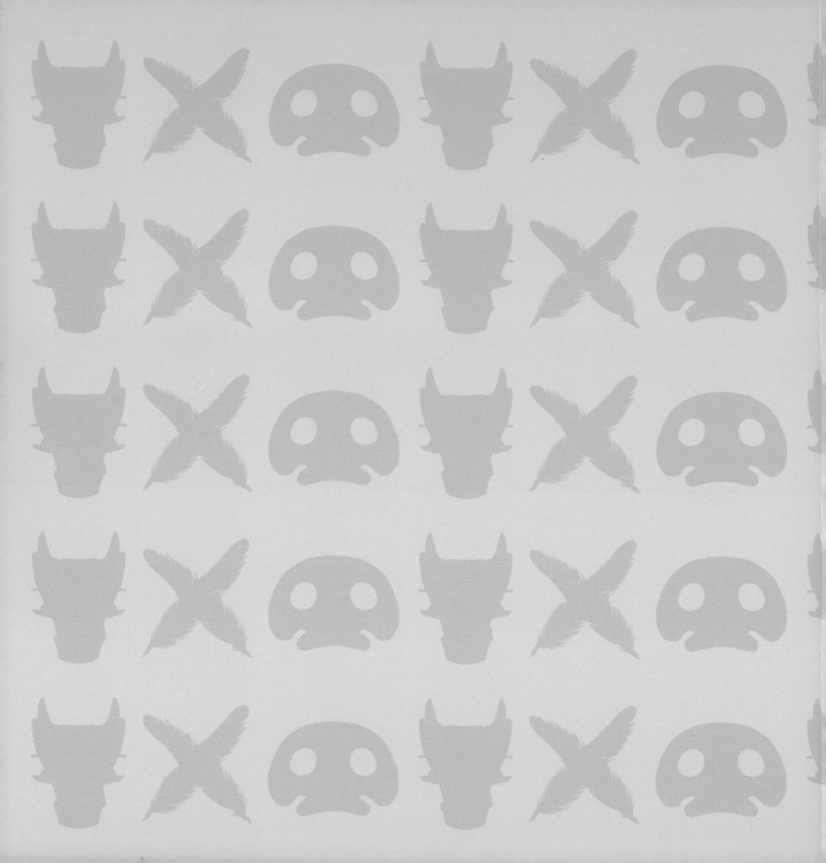